Mitt & Minn at the Wisconsin Cheese Jamboree

by
Kathy-jo Wargin

illustrated by
Karen Busch Holman

All inquiries should be addressed to:
Mitten Press
An imprint of Ann Arbor Media Group LLC
2500 S. State Street
Ann Arbor, MI 48104

Printed and bound by Edwards Brothers, Ann Arbor, Michigan, USA.

10   9   8   7   6   5   4   3   2   1

Library of Congress Cataloging-in-Publication Data

Wargin, Kathy-jo.
Mitt & Minn at the Wisconsin Cheese Jamboree / by Kathy-jo Wargin ;
illustrations by Karen Busch Holman.
p. cm.
Summary: Two white-footed mice, one who lives in Michigan and one
in Minnesota, are both seeking home and family when they meet at a
cheese-eating contest in Wisconsin.
ISBN-13: 978-1-58726-305-7 (hardcover)
ISBN-10: 1-58726-305-X
[1. Adventure and adventurers—Fiction. 2. White-footed mouse—Fiction.
3. Mice—Fiction. 4. Animals—Fiction. 5. Family—Fiction. 6. Middle West—
Fiction.] I. Busch Holman, Karen, 1960- ill. II. Title. III. Title: Mitt and Minn
at the Wisconsin Cheese Jamboree.
PZ7.W234Mir 2007
2006035730

Book design by Somberg Design
www.sombergdesign.com

Contents

Chapter One **Mitt** 5

Chapter Two **Minn** 11

Chapter Three **Floke** 16

Chapter Four **Gota** 24

Chapter Five **Tove the Wood Turtle** 35

Chapter Six **Hulda** 42

Chapter Seven **The Gunflint Trail** 47

Chapter Eight **Grand Marais to Wisconsin** 54

Chapter Nine **Metta** 64

Chapter Ten **Haldor and Henry** 70

Chapter Eleven **Pela and Felka** 76

Chapter Twelve **Wit, Lew, and Kaz** 84

Chapter Thirteen **Sigrid and Stig** 90

Chapter Fourteen **Falda** 101

Chapter Fifteen **Bodil the Vulture** 105

Chapter Sixteen **Minn's Ride** 113

Chapter Seventeen **The Cheese Jamboree** 117

Chapter Eighteen **The Cheese-Eating Contest** 121

Chapter Nineteen **The Barn** 135

Chapter Twenty **Do One Good Thing** 143

Chapter Twenty-One **Mitt and Minn and Lilka** 148

Chapter Twenty-Two **Home** 153

CHAPTER ONE

Mitt

It was early summer and the ranger's station was filled with visitors. The station in the Porcupine Mountains of Michigan had been a good place to stay for a short while, and Mitt had done a good job staying out of sight. Mitt spent most of his time trying to decide the best way to get to Wisconsin, looking over and over again at the bulletin hanging behind the ranger's desk , trying to make sense of it in the careful manner in which most white-footed mice try to make sense of things. But in the end, no matter how many times he looked it over, it still didn't reveal exactly where in Wisconsin he needed to go.

To All Willing:
Heart of Wisconsin Cheese Jamboree
Please Do Come!
One First Prize Cheese Contest
Good Treats and Games
Cheese Smorgasbord,
Try Any Thing You Like!

Even so, he was excited to have been given this much of a clue. It was months ago that he became lost, and the memories of his home in the woods of northern Michigan were becoming faint. Only hints of them remained now, but they were enough to keep him searching. The journey had been long and difficult, and he thought it was nearly over when he was able to meet The Tekla. The Tekla, just as his friend Ruben the moose promised, was a very wise wolverine and would tell Mitt exactly how to get back to his home. Mitt was fond of Ruben and often thought about how much Ruben sacrificed to take him to see The Tekla. Mitt kept repeating The Tekla's advice in his mind.

"You must do one good thing," she had said, "and you will find your way home." When Mitt had begged her to tell him what one good thing that would be, she simply told him that when he saw it, he would know. Mitt remembered the last thing she told him—to a willing heart, nothing is impossible.

The bulletin in the ranger's station must be a clue, thought Mitt. He looked at it again, paying close attention to the words he thought held the most direction.

<u>To</u> <u>A</u>ll <u>Willing</u>:
<u>Heart</u> of Wisconsin Cheese Jamboree
Please **<u>Do</u>** Come!
<u>One</u> First Prize Cheese Contest
<u>Good</u> Treats and Games
Cheese Smorgasbord,
Try Any **<u>Thing</u>** You Like!

But which way to go? How does a little white-footed mouse such as he get to a Cheese Jamboree in Wisconsin?

Mitt squeezed himself into a knothole in the floorboard and dropped into the soft nest he had made out of sawdust and old pieces of cotton. He curled into a ball and tucked his nose beneath his paws. One

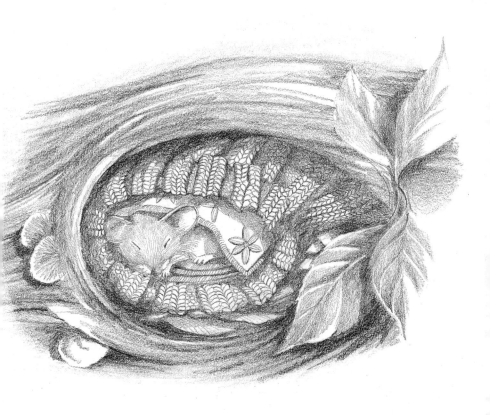

thing was clear. Getting to the Cheese
Jamboree was his chance to do one good
thing. Doing one good thing, The Tekla had
told him, was how he would find his mitten and the way back to his home. Mitt had
been living all alone in the mitten, tucked
into a fallen log in the woods of northern
Michigan, and then one day when Mitt

returned from a party, it was gone. Mitt went to find it, and now he was here, beneath the floorboards of a ranger station wondering how to get to Wisconsin.

Through it all Mitt was sure of one thing— he had to find his way back to his mitten because it was all he had. A long time ago, Mitt woke up by himself in the mitten. His mother and father and sisters and brothers were gone, and he was all by himself. He often thought that perhaps one day his mother and father and sisters and brothers would come back to the mitten and find him there.

CHAPTER TWO

Minn

Minn jumped over a couple of crumbs left behind on the wooden table in the cabin. The crumbs were stale and dry now, too stale for eating, so she decided to play a little game and see how many times she could hop over them.

Playing such a game was a good way to keep her mind off her problem. As she played, the little white-footed mouse began to forget her troubles. That is, until Otso reminded her.

Otso sat in the corner of the log cabin. It was no easy task for him to get in, but the large black bear had nosed his way through a torn window screen and lofted his body over the sill. He liked being in the cabin with Minn, as there were all sorts of different foods to find in Gerdie's pantry.

Gerdie was the only mother Minn had ever known, and Minn recalled how every morning Gerdie told the story of how Minn came to Ely, Minnesota, in a basket of cherries. In return, Minn would tell Gerdie that someday she was going to run off and win a cheese-eating contest.

It was months ago when she had been standing on the dresser and Rink the raven flew in and nabbed her, taking her far away from Gerdie and the cabin. Although she

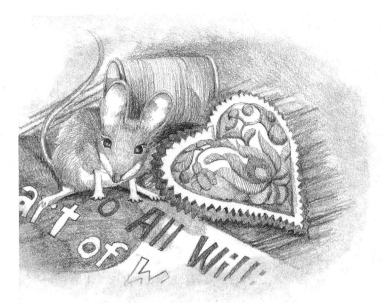

was proud that she had found her way back, she was sad to find the cabin empty with the exception of Paavo the red fox. The words Paavo spoke at that moment were still ringing in her ears, "Gerdie is gone. She's gone to find you."

Gerdie hadn't known that Minn was taken away by Rink, and for months she searched everywhere. When Minn spotted the piece of paper on the dresser and saw it was for a Cheese Jamboree in Wisconsin, it made sense to Minn that perhaps that is why Gerdie was not home to welcome her. Gerdie, thought Minn, was looking for her at the Cheese Jamboree.

To All Willing:
Heart of Wisconsin Cheese Jamboree
Please Do Come!
One First Prize Cheese Contest
Good Treats and Games
Cheese Smorgasbord,
Try Any Thing You Like!

Minn knew she needed to get to the Cheese Jamboree quickly to find Gerdie and tell her to come home. But Minn was scared. She was tired.

As Minn readied herself to embark alone, Otso shook his head back and forth. Otso, using the gestures a bear uses when trying to convey an important message, let Minn know that he did not think she should travel alone. He let her know that Gerdie would be happy to see them both, and that he could be a helpful friend to have on such a long journey. While part of Minn wanted to go alone, the other part wanted some help. Otso moved her along, letting her know that it was early summer in the northland, and if the two of them were going to get to Wisconsin, they better leave now.

As Otso swayed his head back and forth, familiar words began to roll through Minn's mind like musical notes floating through the air on a warm summer day. *Enda barn, kart barn. Enda barn, kart barn.*

Only child, dear child. Those were the words Gerdie used to say to Minn every day. Her soft Swedish accent made each word lilt from Gerdie's lips to Minn's heart. Only child, dear child. "Gerdie loves me," thought Minn, and I'm going to find her and bring her home.

CHAPTER THREE

Floke

The Porcupine Mountains were full and green now with the onset of summer, the leafy trees lush with hushing sounds as the early morning winds ran through them. Mitt thought it would be easy to remain in the park wilderness. There were plenty of crumbs to gather, pieces of bread from campers' sandwiches, peanuts and raisins from bags of trail mix, and small animal-shaped cookies that had fallen out of the hands of young visitors. Mitt thought that if he wanted to, he would never have to leave the ranger's station. He doubted he would ever be discovered there, and even if he was, the ranger seemed like the sort of fellow who wouldn't disagree with a little mouse living below the floorboards.

But even with such promise, a longing in his heart for something he could not define kept him thinking about his mitten and the memories it held. It was time to go. He would make it to Wisconsin and the Cheese Jamboree. Once there, he would win the cheese-eating contest and find his way home. He would be doing the one good thing that The Tekla had told him to do.

Mitt filled his cheek pouches with nuts and crumbs, and squeezed upward out of the knothole. He made certain nobody was around when he did so, and scrambled out a hole in the ranger station's screen door. He raced down the steps and across the stepping stone path and into a thick mess of creeping juniper.

Without being noticed, he put his nose in the air to figure which way to go. Mitt jumped and raced along the forest floor, deciding to find the water he was smelling.

To a willing heart, nothing is impossible he told himself over and over again. Words kept spilling through his mind. Heart of Wisconsin. Cheese Jamboree. Do one good thing.

Mitt reached a place in the forest where a shallow stream seemed to appear from nowhere. He followed the banks through the thick woods until the stream widened a bit. It wasn't long before he noticed the stream webbed into a wide river. The riverbanks were now so far from each other that he could no longer jump across. The water was moving faster too, and sunshine was pouring down through the trees that lined each bank. It was like a tunnel thought Mitt, who paid careful attention to the birds flying above the water. Some were skimming the surface with their feet, grabbing small fish and carrying them away, while others were gliding on air currents, as if they were watching for other choice meals below.

Mitt took a rest beneath a log that was lying by the side of the Presque Isle River.

He nestled himself far beneath it and into a den he made, trying to make sure he was out of view considering all of the birds hovering nearby.

Crickety rick! Crickety rick! Mitt heard a loud, rattling sound coming from over the water. Unsure of what the sound was, he tried not to make a motion and slowly he poked his head out, just far enough to see. Crickety rick! Crickety rick! A large bird in shades of blue and gray with a long bill was hanging over the water. The bird was Floke, and just as Mitt caught a glimpse of her, she plunged into the river and reappeared with a small fish in her bill. She brought the fish to a tree overhanging the river's edge, and began to pound it on the branch where she sat. Oddly, Floke tossed the limp fish back out into the water and watched as four young birds dove at it, missing it each time.

Mitt backed into his den, burrowing a bit deeper beneath the log where he was hiding. Floke was a belted kingfisher, and Mitt knew he didn't want to meet her.

Mitt was trying hard to remain undiscovered when all of a sudden POKE! One of the young kingfishers found him, and being too young to know the difference between a mouse and a dead fish, began to needle Mitt with his bill.

Poke! Poke!

Mitt kept backing into his den, not realizing that the more he backed into it, the more his backside was coming out from beneath the other side of the log. Before he knew it, he was out in the open and surrounded by four baby kingfishers.

Their sharp bills pecking at him and clumsy feet stepping on him, the baby kingfishers were delighted to find a mouse. Mitt began to squeal, which caught the attention of their mother. In a flash Floke was there, her eyes beaded in on Mitt, her head feathers straight up in the air.

Mitt could think only one thing—this was the end.

CHAPTER FOUR

Gota

Minn sat upon the piece of paper. I can do this, she thought. I can win a cheese-eating contest, and Gerdie will find me there.

Minn climbed up on Otso's back, and the pair began their journey east through the wilderness of northern Minnesota.

Otso knew which paths to take to lead them out of Ely without being noticed. Nothing would bother Minn as long as she was with a big black bear like Otso, but there were things that could bother Otso. It was early summer and visitors were beginning to camp and canoe all throughout the Boundary Waters Canoe Area Wilderness. Although many people looked forward to seeing a real bear in the wilderness, often times city people would take one look at Otso and holler. Some city people would try to feed Otso, and that wasn't good either, because Otso was the one who always got in trouble when they did.

All along the way Otso did his best to stay out of sight. With Minn perched on his back, he walked along the dense edges of small lakes, and they wondered along footpaths made by voyageurs and native people a long time ago. Their days were filled with long naps and plenty of food, and soon the pair reached the Gunflint Trail and began to follow it southward.

One evening as the pair bedded down in a cradle of jagged rocks near a stream, Otso fell asleep quickly while Minn remained awake. As Otso slept, Minn heard a voice. She was laying quietly in his paws when she heard, "Who cooks for you? Who cooks for you?" She did not know who was saying this, but she knew it did one thing—it made her hungry.

Minn thought about the question and answered to herself that Gerdie cooks for her. Gerdie cooked and fed her delightful treats every day, and Minn, growing hungrier still, ventured into the woods to find a little treat for herself. As she scampered

through new unfurled ferns and blue violets, she kept hearing, "Who cooks for you? Who cooks for you?" As she was listening, a flurry of feathers came upon her and knocked her away from the safety of the underbrush. She found herself looking straight into the eyes of a barred owl.

"Who cooks for you? Who cooks for you?" The owl was Gota, and he kept asking the same question but Minn wasn't sure how to answer. She didn't like the thought of talking about dinner with an owl, because mice are most often dinner FOR an owl.

Minn thought of only one thing to say.

"Knock, knock."
Gota looked at Minn before answering, "Who's there?"
"Repeat," answered Minn.
"Repeat who?" Gota responded.

"Okay, then," said Minn—"Whoooo. Whoooo. Whoooo."

The owl looked at Minn. He liked her and decided not to eat her. Instead, he decided to tell her a story.

"Long ago, the world was always dark. It was night all the time. The Great Hare was walking through the woods, and it was very hard for him to see his way. Even though it was dark, he was able to see the saw-whet owl perched on a branch. 'Owl,' he said, 'I don't like it to be dark. I think I will make it be daylight.' The owl thought about this and told the Great Hare that he doubted if the hare was strong enough to make daylight. The owl said, 'Okay, then, if you want it to be light, and I want it to be dark, let us have a contest and see who wins. The winner will get his way.'

"The Great Hare thought this was a very good idea, as he was sure he would win. Soon, the pair was joined by all the other forest animals. Some of the animals liked it to be dark, and some liked the daylight.

"The contest began with the Great Hare calling out 'Light! Light!' And saw-whet owl saying, 'Night! Night!' If one of them should call out the other's word by mistake, they would lose.

"'Light, light!' called Great Hare. 'Night, night!' called the saw-whet owl. The animals cheered back and forth for the one they wanted to win. All of a sudden, owl called out the Great Hare's word, 'Light!' by mistake.

"The Great Hare was happy that he won, and delighted that it would be daylight all the time. But when he looked at all of the other animals who had cheered for night because they needed it and saw the look on the saw-whet owl's face, he decided that perhaps they could still have both, and that is why there are day and night."

Minn enjoyed the story very much and wanted Gota to keep talking with her. However, the barred owl simply looked Minn in the eyes and said, "I will not eat you, but in return please promise me that you will remember this story. You may need it on your journey."

"My journey?" Minn asked. "How do you know I'm on a journey?" By the time Minn finished, Gota was gone. In the distance Minn heard all sorts of hooting and whoo-ing and calling and flapping. The forest was busy at nighttime, and Minn thought about all of the animals that needed dark-ness for their cover.

Just as Minn turned around to leave,

WHOOSH; a northern goshawk came down upon her and scooped her up. She called for Otso with high-pitched cries, but Otso was sound asleep and unable to hear her over the other sounds of the forest. Firmly in the clutch of the goshawk's talons, Minn was being squeezed nearly to death.

CHAPTER FIVE
Tove the Wood Turtle

Back in Michigan, Floke was staring straight at Mitt while the young ones made their fuss all around him. The mother was considering taking Mitt up to her perch so that her young ones would have a chance to learn how to eat a mouse. Mitt looked around slowly and carefully, realizing he had nowhere to go. The river current was too strong and he knew he might be swept away for good if he jumped in. Even so, it was his only hope, so he was starting to edge himself in that direction when SLAM!

The lights went out.

Mitt had no idea what had happened. All he knew was that something was on top of him, and he had no idea what it was. It felt hard and smooth at the same time, and when he pushed against it, it seemed to go nowhere. He could hear the muffled sounds of the kingfishers calling Keee! Keee! Keee! at one another, but with every call they seemed to be moving farther away.

Mitt tried to lift the heavy object but it would not rise. He tried to make loud noises, but the sound went nowhere. He moaned and groaned and turned and squirmed. Mitt suddenly realized he was under a turtle and the turtle wouldn't move. It was not very comfortable beneath the shell of such a big turtle, so Mitt did the only thing he could think to do. He began to tickle the wood turtle. He took his little paw and wiggled it right in the corner where the turtle's leg was coming out of the shell, and tickled him until he began to raise himself up.

The moment he did, Mitt raced out from beneath the turtle.

The turtle was Tove and, having no idea that a mouse had been beneath him, introduced himself to Mitt.

"Hello there, young fellow, are you new around here?"

Mitt began to explain that he was on his way to a Cheese Jamboree in Wisconsin, and how he was told that if he could do one good thing he would find his way home again. He told Tove how he lost his mitten

in the first place, and how hard it had been to get this far.

Tove, being old and slow and thoughtful, looked at Mitt and said, "I thought you looked a little naked without your home. Is it like mine? I haven't lost mine yet. You really need to be more responsible with your things, little fellow."

Mitt was exasperated by this and so simply asked him, "Can you help me get to Wisconsin?"

"Oh, certainly. Why didn't you say so in the first place?"

Mitt waited. "Okay, then, tell me."

Tove began, "What has a mouth but doesn't eat?"

Mitt was puzzled. "You said you would tell me how to get to Wisconsin. You just asked me a question."

But Tove continued, "What has a bed but doesn't sleep?"

Mitt looked around. He didn't answer and was growing impatient with Tove's game.

Tove spoke again, "What waves but has no hands?"

Mitt didn't know whether he liked Tove or not. His old face was weathered and gentle-looking, but Mitt couldn't understand why the turtle was asking questions when he said he would tell him how to get to Wisconsin. Tove was old, thought Mitt, and wise in the games of woodland life, so Mitt decided to respect the turtle and try to answer the questions.

"What has a mouth but doesn't eat? And a bed but doesn't sleep? What waves but has no hands?" Mitt thought quietly to himself. Mitt put his face into his paws and sat on the riverbank. Tove didn't offer the answers to Mitt. He just stood there, waiting for Mitt to earn it on his own.

"A mouth, a bed, and waves?" thought Mitt. As Mitt sat there thinking, a river otter jumped out of the water and onto the bank and landed right in front of Tove. "I've got it!" cried Mitt. "A river!"

The river otter was Hulda, and she began to chirp at Tove.

"I can't believe you are making him answer that dumb little river riddle. Don't you know any new riddles? That one is getting so old, Tove!"

At first Mitt didn't know whether or not Tove and Hulda were friends, but then Tove spoke.

"The mouse will need to know a little bit about the river if he's going to take the river to Wisconsin," said Tove. "I was just making sure he was ready."

And so Tove told Mitt that Hulda would take him along the river, and Mitt climbed upon Hulda's back. It seemed an unlikely way to find Wisconsin, but what choice did he have?

CHAPTER SIX

Hulda

Mitt grasped Hulda's dense undercoat, hanging on to the longer outer hairs so that he wouldn't fall off as Hulda made her way south. The woods were thick in places, so thick that Mitt forgot it was daylight. Hulda was good at navigating the river, and when the water became too fast or rocky or difficult, she would lope over the banks and run alongside the trail, staying out of sight.

It took many days for the pair to travel south. During that time, Mitt told Hulda all about his journey to find his mitten and return home to northern Michigan. He explained how The Tekla told him that if he would do one good thing, he would find his way home. He told how he spotted the bulletin for the Cheese Jamboree at the ranger's station and knew it must be a sign. Indeed, it was a sign, for when he read it he knew it meant that the one good thing he could do would be to win a cheese-eating contest.

Hulda took this in stride and listened to Mitt chatter much in the way an older sister listens to a young brother talk without stopping.

The pair had traveled for a long time when one night, the clouds began to roll in deep dense shades of purple and black. The storm started as a light rain, and when the lightning and thunder began, the raindrops came down in sheets. Hulda was wise enough to take refuge in an old log pile, and inside, she covered Mitt to keep him warm and dry.

Mitt took the opportunity to ask Hulda how long it would be before they reached Wisconsin. "How far are we?" he asked.

But it was too late for such questions. Hulda was fast asleep, and Mitt was not. As he drew in the mix of Hulda's sweet musky scent and raindrops on the pine needle floor, Mitt heard footsteps outside.

"Hulda, wake up. I hear something," whispered Mitt.

It was a young coyote, and he wanted to get at Hulda. He stuck his nose into the den and began to scratch away at the shelter with his paws. Hulda began to scream high-pitched noises. The storm was still raging when all of a sudden CRACK! Lightning hit the forest floor not far from the log pile.

Now the rain was so heavy that it was hard to tell the difference between the riverbank and the forest floor. The coyote began to chase Hulda, and Hulda slipped into the raging water. She was calling for Mitt to hide and wait, but Mitt could not hear her through the thunder and falling rain. Mitt followed after Hulda, and unable to see where he was in the storm, fell into the river and was quickly pulled away by the swift current and heavy waves.

Struggling with all his might, Mitt knew there was no way out.

CHAPTER SEVEN

The Gunflint Trail

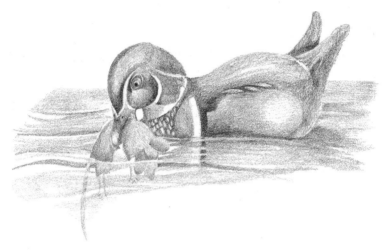

Meanwhile, in Minnesota, the northern goshawk was making its way through the woods with Minn in his grasp. He had nestlings back home, and their mother had sent him out to find food for them. He wasn't having much luck, but then he spotted the little mouse. Although it wasn't much to feed them, at least it was something.

The goshawk was large and had red eyes, and a hooked bill that gave it a menacing smile. He had Minn so firmly in his talons that Minn could barely breathe, let alone wiggle herself free from his grasp.

The goshawk flew quickly; its wings beating in such a way that it made the same noise as rain falling on a drum. It had a long way to go to get back to its nest of sticks and branches clustered in the old pine tree.

The bird flew south along the corridor of the Gunflint Trail, veering left and right and up and down.

At the same time, Mitt struggled against the current, splashing and waving his paws back and forth, trying not to be pulled under by the strong river current. Hulda was gone and although Mitt was alone, he was happy that Hulda had escaped the coyote.

The current swept Mitt toward shore and near a raft of ducks waiting near the bank for the storm to break. But the water was still coursing, and Mitt was growing weak. Mitt found himself being pulled under by the current. In a flash, he was underwater.

The next thing Mitt felt was the gentle pull around his middle as he was being lifted out of the water. Wedged in the bill of a large wood duck, Mitt was limp from exhaustion. Somehow, in the mysterious way that animals know such things, the wood duck took Mitt to a hole in an old tree. The hole was the duck's home, and it was warm and dry inside. The wood duck placed Mitt gently in the grasses that lined the bed, and laid right next to him as he went to sleep.

The next morning, the darkness of the storm was like the memory of a very bad dream, and Mitt scarcely remembered all that had happened. He knew Hulda was gone; he knew he almost drowned. He knew he spent the night sleeping to the soft rhythm of Kerr the wood duck's breathing and he felt safe and warm.

When he woke later in the morning, Mitt told Kerr all about his mitten and his quest for Wisconsin. Kerr was on his own quest too, for now that his nestlings had hatched and were being raised by their mother, there wasn't much use for him around the nest. He knew, in the way that most ducks know, that he was to meet up with other ducks in a new territory and wait for the summer molting to happen. But Kerr liked the secure sounds and smells of a nest filled with young ones and was happy to have Mitt there. Kerr was familiar with Wisconsin and had flown there before, and so he decided that he would take Mitt the rest of the way.

Back in Minnesota, the goshawk was still in flight along the Gunflint Trail, now following a portion of road where cars often traveled. As the bird kept Minn tight in his grasp, he spotted a snowshoe hare below. The hare sensed the bird and made a dash along the side of the road.

The goshawk pursued the hare, which decided to follow the road right into town. And then it happened. The hare, nervously darting back and forth deeper into the town of Grand Marais, stopped at the waterfront, giving the goshawk his chance.

The goshawk didn't realize they had caused such a commotion, stirring up a flock of herring gulls. All at once the gulls were midair and squawking, disrupting the goshawk so much that he couldn't grasp the hare, and he let go of Minn while trying to do so.

Minn was dropped on a dock while the goshawk flew away. Minn could sense one thing—a busy dock in the middle of summer was no place for a mouse to land.

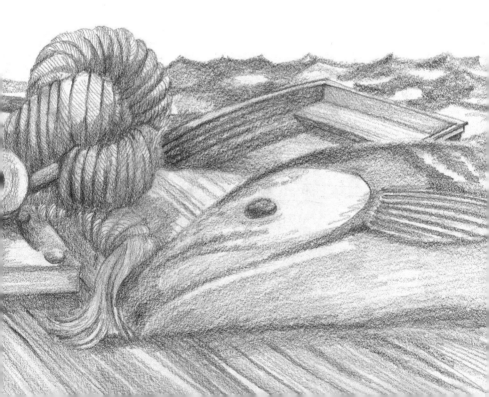

CHAPTER EIGHT

Grand Marais to Wisconsin

Minn had been dropped onto the dock so hard that she was stunned and couldn't move. Her light brown fur blended into the light brown aging of the planks, and so the harbormaster did not see her there as he continued sweeping back and forth.

Minn saw the broom coming her way and knew if she was knocked into the water she would surely drown. Then it happened.

At the same time, Mitt and Kerr the wood duck had reached a small town called Rhinelander, Wisconsin.

"I'm in Wisconsin!" shouted Mitt. "I've made it!"

Then Kerr asked Mitt, "So where is the Cheese Jamboree?

"In Wisconsin," answered Mitt in the stead-fast way that a mouse who knows what he's talking about will answer.

"But where in Wisconsin?" asked Kerr.

"Where there is cheese," said Mitt, smugly.

Kerr covered his laughter, not wanting to
discourage his friend. "Mitt," said Kerr,
"this is Wisconsin. The whole place is
cheese."

Mitt hadn't known that Wisconsin was so
big, or that there would be so many places
for cheese.

Kerr heard the other ducks calling for him and felt a pull between staying with Mitt or doing what nature was moving him to do. Mitt realized this, and knew what he had to say. "You go, Kerr. I'll find the Jamboree. I'll be okay."

And with that, Kerr left.

Mitt poked around his new surroundings. There were old log buildings and the aroma of wood smoke, and people were laughing and talking loudly. Some were carrying small logs and placing them in piles, while others were swinging axes back and forth. Mitt was very hungry and followed his nose into the building that seemed to hold the most promise for food.

"This is a wonderful place for a mouse," thought Mitt. The floorboards had plenty of holes and gaps for hiding, and even the walls had nooks and crannies for climbing and napping. It smelled like sweet cream butter and wood smoke and bacon and fried potatoes, and there were plates of cookies set in pairs all the way down a very long table.

Mitt took his time walking across the long table, going from one plate of

cookies to the next, then on to a bright
blue bowl filled with biscuits. There were
glasses of milk set out in a rows, too, and
little cloths scattered here and there. Mitt
liked that, because he could scramble
beneath one should he need to hide.

Content in the way that most mice will be while eating cookies, Mitt's cheeks were filling to the point they could hold no more when he began to hear humming. The soft humming turned to quiet singing, and the singing turned into hearty laughter. The woman's voice was loud in a happy sort of way, laughing and singing at the same time while she pounded mounds of dough onto a wooden slab.

Mitt drew closer. "Maybe she can tell me where the Cheese Jamboree is," thought Mitt.

He took one step, then two, then all of a sudden WHAM! From right behind Mitt came the blow of a rolling pin, hitting the table with a thwack.

"Otto!" cried the woman, "It's just a little mouse."

"But Trula," said the man, "we can't have a mouse here in the logging camp. It'll eat all the goodies before the men get a chance!"

Trula laughed. "Out with you, Otto. You leave that mouse be—if you touch him I will serve him to you in your next slice of pie!"

Mitt wasn't sure if he liked the sound of that and began to back himself away, only to find himself caught by the tail. He curled himself upward to have a look. It was Trula.

"Well, hello there little darling, you like my cookies?" she said. "You're cold, my darling, let's warm you up some."

Trula placed Mitt into a big ceramic bowl with a heavy cotton cloth inside. She placed the bowl just the right distance away from the cookstove—close enough to warm the bowl, but not so close that it cooked Mitt.

Settled, Mitt took a short, deep nap to the sounds of Trula working. When the loggers came in she fed them well, and they thanked her by taking second helpings. Trula knew she had the most important job of all, because if the men did not eat well, they wouldn't work well.

When the men left, their heavy boots boomed upon the wooden floor, causing enough of a thunder that it raised Mitt out of the bowl. He thought to ask Trula, in the thoughtful way a grateful mouse should ask, if she knew anything about the Cheese Jamboree.

"I know all about the Cheese Jamboree," said Trula to Mitt who was hanging along the side of the bowl now. "It's a long way from here but it's not impossible to get there. When you get up in the mornin', I will give you a nice breakfast and send you on your way."

That night, after all the men were fed and Trula closed the kitchen and went home, Mitt fell asleep knowing that in the morning, he would set off for the Jamboree.

But he didn't know that in the middle of night, there would be a change in plans.

Metta

Back on the dock in Minnesota, the broom came scraping toward Minn with two short swishes, followed by one long swish. Its fibers were brisk against the weathered wood and made a gentle scraping sound.

The harbormaster neared Minn, who was still so stunned by her fall that she couldn't move. The broom kept coming closer when Whoosh! Minn went flying through the air as the broom hit her, sending her right off the dock. Minn was falling into Lake Superior, knowing that such a fall would be the end of her.

Then she hit with a thud.

The boat she had fallen into belonged to Metta and was just leaving the safe harbor of Grand Marais.

"Why, look at you," the girl shouted through the wind. Minn couldn't tell if she was a young girl or a grown girl, as she looked somewhere in between. Metta picked Minn up and then quickly put her down again, just in time to catch the rope she was working to keep the small sailboat on course.

Minn knew in the way a well-traveled mouse knows things that Metta would be kind to her, and so she climbed up near her to watch.

"Isn't being out on the open water the best feeling there is?" Metta asked.

Minn listened. And when she felt strong enough to speak, in the way that she could do, she told Metta all about Gerdie and Otso, and how she needed to get to the Cheese Jamboree in Wisconsin.

"Well I'm going to Bayfield, Wisconsin, and that's not too far from the Jamboree," Metta boasted. "I will take you there!"

Minn watched Metta closely and thought she was an expert sailor. She kept the boat upright and steady as the wind pushed them along. They stayed near the shore as best they could, and Metta said it was a

perfect day for sailing. Metta shared meals of soda crackers and orange pop, peanut butter and bananas. Minn thought Metta looked very pretty as she held the white ropes in her freckled hands, her blond hair pulled back in a long ponytail to keep it off her face.

They sailed all day and into early evening, and as the sun began to set, Metta grew very excited about the islands they were about to reach. "Oh, there are so many of them," she blurted out to Minn. "I just love the challenge. Don't you love challenges?"

Before Minn had a chance to answer, a loud boat with two red pontoons and a grey cabin came carefully up to the sailboat.

"Are you Metta Johanssen?" the voice boomed over a loudspeaker. "Your parents are very worried." The boat came closer and a man with a jacket that said U.S.

Coast Guard spoke kindly but firmly to Metta. "Young lady, you are not qualified to be out here by yourself. Your parents are very worried. We are going to take you in to them."

With that, the Coast Guard pulled down the sails and tied her boat to theirs, and escorted her up and into their boat. Minn was very frightened when Metta left her all alone on the sailboat. Metta was gone and the boat was speeding along now, pulled by the Coast Guard boat, bumping up and down rather rigorously in the water. Waves splashed over the sides and Minn hid herself in Metta's brown paper bag of food and closed her eyes. It would be a long ride.

CHAPTER TEN

Haldor and Henry

That night, as Minn was on Metta's boat, which was being pulled to shore by the Coast Guard, Mitt heard a creaking noise come from somewhere in the cook shanty where he was sleeping.

Creeeeeeeek. Then nothing. Creeeeeek. The sound grew a little bit louder and then faded into nothing.

Mitt decided that perhaps it was the wind causing two tree branches to rub together and so he closed his eyes.

The ceramic bowl by the cookstove was a cozy bed, and so Mitt began to breathe deeply and soundly in the way that a mouse trying to fall back to sleep in the middle of the night will do.

But as he did so, something felt different. A moist, foglike warmth came over him—the type of warmth Mitt knew didn't belong to a campfire or a cookstove.

Mitt opened his eyes to find himself nose to nose with Haldor. Haldor was the resident lynx of the logging camp, and he had come for one reason—to get Mitt. The lynx had his face right to the edge of the bowl and was opening his mouth, ready to swallow. Mitt jumped out of the bowl and scrammed up the wall where, much to his surprise, the lynx followed. The log walls were rough enough to provide traction for Mitt as well as the big cat, which was not far behind.

Engaged in the chase, Haldor sneered, "I like this game of cat and mouse, don't you?"

Mitt didn't answer; he just kept racing up and down the walls trying to escape Haldor's sharp teeth.

Mitt darted out the door with Haldor's great big paws pouncing down upon his tail every now and again. Mitt disappeared into the forest under the cover of night. He raced through the woods while Haldor continued after him. Mitt could hear the big cat panting, and every once in awhile he would make a screeching catlike noise that made Mitt shiver from the tip of his nose to

the end of his tail. Every few steps Haldor was gaining measure on him, forcing Mitt to run faster and faster.

Mitt, now wise in the ways of people as well as animals, spotted a yard light and thought perhaps there could be a building nearby in which to hide. He ran toward it, Haldor getting closer still. All of a sudden the lynx leaped up in the air and was about to land on Mitt when an "AAAAYE!" came from the darkness.

The stout man hollering was Henry, and he was startled to see such a big lynx running across his driveway on a dark, early summer morning. Haldor was startled and knew enough to keep his distance from the man, and so he quickly turned tail and leapt back into the woods, leaving Mitt laying exhausted at Henry's feet.

Henry grabbed Mitt and cradled him in his

hands. Mitt's body was trembling with every breath, and not knowing what was going to happen next, he closed his eyes. But much to Mitt's surprise, Henry took him inside the truck and placed him on the seat right next to him and left for work. He made a little bed out of a handkerchief and settled Mitt into it carefully. "Believe you me," said Henry, "that cat would have got you for sure!" Mitt was too weak to answer and so he didn't, but somewhere deep inside, he knew it was true.

As he lay there, Mitt whimpered in a sad and tired way. He would not see Trula in the morning and get directions to the Cheese Jamboree. Now he was dead-tired in a truck with a man named Henry with no idea where they were going.

CHAPTER ELEVEN
Pela and Felka

Minn felt the boat bump up against the rocky shore as it was pulled onto the land. It made a terrible scraping noise as the bottom rubbed against the earth, and it jostled her back and forth in the paper sack.

From a distance, she heard cries of happiness mixed with words of frustration from

Metta's family as they greeted her. Before Minn knew it, Metta's father was cleaning out the boat so he could dock it in the Bayfield Marina. All of a sudden, the sack was being thrown through the air and into a big smelly messy garbage can. Thinking it best to stay out of sight, Minn waited until all the voices had cleared, although she really wanted to tell Metta goodbye.

Once quiet on shore, Minn crawled out of the garbage can and slid down its greasy side to land on a piece of lawn. But before she had a chance to gather her wits, she was being poked in the belly by two ducks.

The ducks were Pela and Felka, and they were shouting at her, "Hey you, when do ducks get up?" Minn didn't answer. She didn't know they had been sleeping right near the can and she had woken them from their huddled nap. "We said, hey you, when do ducks get up?" Minn shrugged her shoulders and as she did, the larger of the two spoke up and said, "At the quack of dawn!"

The pair laughed heartily while Minn sat quietly.

"Oh, I see we have a serious mouse problem." And the ducks laughed even harder.

They didn't stop picking on poor Minn. They poked with their bills, and they tried holding her tail down with their webbed feet.

"Hey you," the smaller one said. "What do ducks eat with their soup?" And before Minn caught on, Pela answered "Quackers!"

It was obvious to Minn that Pela and Felka thought they were pretty funny, but she did not like them at all, as they kept poking and pulling at her. She tried to spot

a place to hide, but there was none. Felka picked Minn up with his bill and began to waddle around the park. By this time, Minn had it with them and so hollered, "What type of ducks are you anyway?"

"We're dabblers," snipped Pela. Minn, now irritated to the point of no return replied in haste, "Oh, is that right? Did you say babblers? Oh yes, I can see you are indeed babblers!"

Pela and Felka could not believe that a small mouse would dare try to outdo them in such a way. Felka still had Minn in his bill, and so Pela told him to start flying. Felka did so, and Pela was right behind. "This will be the end of you, mouse!"

Minn thought that perhaps, this time, it would be.

Meanwhile, Mitt began to warm up as the gentle hum of the old truck soothed him. They were making their way down the dirt road as the sun was just beginning to poke up from the horizon. Henry was smiling and listening to the radio, his big hands holding the steering wheel and every so often stroking Mitt.

The truck chortled and rattled when it came to a stop, pulling Mitt out of the dreamlike rest he had been taking. Henry took his work cap off and set Mitt inside, carrying him into the paper mill. "I'll make sure you eat and you drink today little fellow, and you'll be feeling better soon."

Mitt was too weak from the lynx episode to disagree, and so kept sleeping in Henry's hat, the bright lights and loud din of the mill proving no distraction. As the morning burned on, other workers would come in and take quick looks at Mitt, and every so often Mitt heard Henry tell them to let the little guy sleep.

When Mitt woke, Henry was gone. Mitt looked around and could not spot him anywhere. He was hungry now, and felt he would be safe if he went in search of a few leftover lunch crumbs. He went cautiously out of the cap and down the table. He was following his nose along the workshop floor when WHAM! He had walked onto a platform stacked with boxes and had not realized it. The pallet was being loaded onto a truck and, in an instant, the truck gate came down, shutting Mitt into its cargo hold. And then the truck began to move.

The truck was carrying a load of toilet paper, and Mitt was stuck inside. He hollered and whined in the way that a scared mouse will do, but it was no use.

Mitt steadied himself on top of a box

during the ride, which seemed awfully long. It wasn't until the truck came to a stop that he heard voices. There were two men inside, and Mitt heard one say to the other, "We're here, the frozen tundra at last!"

Mitt sobbed. He would never survive on a frozen tundra. He would be left in the snow and freeze to death. There would be no food. There would be no other animals. He would never get to the Cheese Jamboree. He would never find his home.

When the gate went up, Mitt didn't bother to look. He simply bolted for the first hint of cover he could find.

CHAPTER TWELVE

Wit, Lew, and Kaz

"Whew! That was close," Mitt said out loud.

"What was close?"

Mitt was too scared to look to see where the voice was coming from. But before he knew it, three figures were standing right in front of him.

"I said, what was close?"

The three mice waited for Mitt to answer. Mitt wasn't sure what to say, and so waited for a moment. Thinking he was alone and left on the frozen tundra, he decided that perhaps these mice would be the last living creatures he would see. He decided to tell them his story, just so that at least somebody somewhere would know he tried to do one good thing. And so there in the dark shadows of an unfamiliar place, he told three strangers all about his journey and his quest for home.

The mice listened. Their names were Wit, Lew, and Kaz, and they hung on every

word that Mitt told them, that is, until he got to the part about feeling so sad that he had been left on the frozen tundra to die.

"But you're not on the frozen tundra right now," exclaimed Wit. "You're near it, but you're not on it. We know all about the frozen tundra."

The three nodded in agreement while Lew, the chubbiest and slowest speaking, added, "We should know all about it, we're cheddarheads."

"Cheddarhead mice?" Mitt had never heard of cheddarhead mice. He knew of white-footed mice and deer mice, harvest mice, jumping mice, meadow mice, and such, but he had never heard of cheddarhead mice.

At that, Wit, Lew, and Kaz began to laugh in the way that hearty mice will laugh at others who aren't cheddarheads. They went on to explain, "A cheddarhead loves cheese and football and potato chips and bratwurst and noise and friends." Wit and Lew tackled Kaz while they were talking.

Mitt thought it sounded like fun to be a cheddarhead, and so asked the question that any mouse would ask if in a similar situation. "Can I be one, too?"

This threw Wit, Lew, and Kaz into a fit of laughter, although Mitt did not see what was so funny. "Of course you can't be a cheddarhead."

"Why not?" Mitt begged.

"Because you're from Michigan!" they all roared in a fit of laughter. Then Wit spoke up, "Ah, it's not so bad little fellow, at least you're not from Minnesota!"

"Yeah, or Chicago!" added Lew.

The three laughed even harder at that, and Mitt, not knowing why he should laugh, joined in, because it just seemed that everything with Wit, Lew, and Kaz seemed fun.

Then, realizing in the way that mice will realize their hunger, Wit, Lew, and Kaz raced through one long hallway and into a vent that took them into a long winding tunnel. They urged Mitt to follow, and having such a good time with his new friends, he saw no problem in doing so.

All along the way they picked up pieces of food that had been left behind. The janitor had not swept yet, and so leftover pieces of hot dog buns and nacho chips were easy to find.

As the four were scrambling around filling their cheeks, Wit had an idea. "Okay fellows, we're getting this guy to the Cheese Jamboree. Follow me. We're taking him out to the tundra."

"The tundra? I don't want to go to the tundra," Mitt thought to himself. This time, Mitt wasn't sure if he should follow, but what choice did he have?

CHAPTER THIRTEEN

Sigrid and Stig

The duck Felka still had Minn tightly in his bill as he was flying south. He was sour inside because Minn had met his barbing with equal insults of her own, and the pair were not off to a good start. And so Felka had decided he was going to give Minn one last teasing.

The duck reached Hayward quickly, and once there, he intended to drop Minn into the mouth of a fish that was larger than an airplane and setting on the ground. Its mouth was open wide and Minn could tell it had

already eaten people as they were standing in its mouth, waiting to go down the rest of the way. The duck came in real close to the fish's mouth and said, as he dropped her, "We'll see whose babbling now, little mousie!"

Minn could feel herself spinning into the mouth of the gigantic muskie, and could do nothing but close her eyes and think her last thoughts. Then it went dark.

Minn woke to the sounds of footsteps and people talking. She had missed the mouth of the fish and landed in a nearby wild rose bush. It broke her fall but, even so, she lost her breath and had to rest for a few moments. It was mid morning now and people were everywhere. So Minn decided that the best place to stay would be the patch of woods she spotted nearby. There were yellow birch and sugar maple, white pine and balsam fir to hide in. It was a lovely mix of greens and grays, and Minn thought it looked like a quiet place to build up her strength.

She nestled into a light brown patch that was soft and seemed warm beneath the sunlight. It was the perfect bed, curling around her more as she laid herself into it, causing her to quickly fall asleep in the gentle morning sunlight.

She barely heard the sound of dry twigs breaking beneath the feet of the mother deer coming closer. The sound was faint and light, but it was just loud enough that it caused Minn to stir and pay attention.

All of a sudden, the warm blanket where Minn was nestled began to move, and the mother doe greeted her fawn with gentle licking and happy tail swishing. The doe was Sigrid, and she noticed Minn in the way that nature makes all mothers take

notice of small creatures in need. Her nostrils let Minn know that she was a friend, and she put her large wet tongue upon Minn's head.

"And what do we have here?" asked Sigrid. The fawn hadn't noticed Minn's presence yet and was surprised at the discovery. But even so, Minn could tell the fawn was delighted to have her there.

Minn began to tell Sigrid about Gerdie and her search for the Cheese Jamboree. Sigrid was familiar with the ways of the woods as well as the ways of man and cars and small animals, and knew how important it is that all young animals be with their mothers. Sigrid lowered her head so that Minn could climb up and take hold of the longer hairs between her ears. She said in the way that a mother deer will say that she would take Minn to Gerdie. She didn't say how she would do this, but Minn felt safe with Sigrid and didn't need to ask. Then, urging her fawn to follow, she began a quiet walk through the forest. It was coming on late summer now, and the Solomon's seal and dewberry were thick in places. Minn was happy and peaceful riding through such a beautiful place with Sigrid and the fawn. It reminded her of how Gerdie took such good care of her in the woods near Ely, and how much she wanted to be with her at home once more.

That night, as the sun fell and the forest became shades of dusk between night and day, Sigrid nosed a bed in the tall brush and curled around her fawn. She let Minn tuck in between them, and the three looked out over the forest. Sigrid rested in the way that a caring mother will rest, alert to the sounds in the forest, and yet calm enough to let her fawn fall into a deep and restful sleep.

"I'm bringing you to Stig, and he will bring you to your mother," Sigrid whispered as the three lay there huddled and hiding. "I can't take you myself, because my fawn is too small and we can't travel that far. I must stay here where there is food and where I am familiar with the places I can hide her. You could stay with me, but I know how important it is for you to be with your mother, and I know how worried she must be. A long time ago it was much harder for us to take care of our fawns, and many were lost. The memory of that time in nature was passed to me through my ancestors. It was what my mother learned from her mother, and so on. Because of this, I will never let anything happen to my fawn, or you."

Minn let Sigrid know, in the way that a lost mouse will do, that she wanted to know what happened so long ago, but was afraid to ask. Sigrid, sensing that a lost mouse might want to hear such a story, began.

"A long time ago, fawns were born without spots. They were easy prey to catch because they did not blend into the woods like they should. Many young deer were caught by predators or chased far away. One day, a very strong doe went to the Great Spirit and said, 'You have given bears great strength so that they may survive. You have given wolves sharp teeth so they may always protect themselves. You have given beavers flat tails and webbed feet so they may swim well underwater. You have given porcupines quills so they may always defend themselves.' And then while putting her fawn before him, the mother deer asked the Great Spirit, 'What about us? What about our babies and how will you help us protect them?'

"The Great Spirit listened to this mother and agreed that the fawn too should have protection. In an instant, he made paint from the earth's surface and painted the fawn with spots so he could blend into the forest and escape the eyes of predators. Then he breathed upon that same fawn, taking away its smell, so no other animals would find it in the forest."

Sigrid continued. "That is why our babies have spots so we can hide them, and no smell so no other animals will bother them. We are grateful to the Great Spirit, and so do our best

to take care of our babies—and others, too."

Minn fell asleep after listening to Sigrid's story. In the morning Sigrid brought Minn to a large buck who seemed fond of Sigrid and her fawn. Sigrid told the buck, in the way that gentle mother's will do, Minn's story and where she needed to go. The buck nodded, and Sigrid turned around to leave, quickly disappearing into the understory.

Before Minn knew it, she was tossed up onto the buck's antlers and the pair were dashing through the forest, crashing down small trees and bushes and leaping over little streams. Minn held on as tightly as she could, and the buck carried her forward.

CHAPTER FOURTEEN
Falda

Wit, Lew, and Kaz nudged Mitt in between them and forced him down the corridor to the frozen tundra. Mitt wasn't sure why they would do such a thing after they had been such enjoyable friends. They pushed and prodded him along, and Mitt could not fight back. All of a sudden they were out of the darkness and into the light overlooking a wide stretch of green. Wit announced, "The frozen tundra, my friend, is your ticket home."

It was not at all what Mitt was thinking it would be. There was no snow or ice or wind. It was as pleasant as a summer day, and Mitt was confused.

Lew chimed in, "This is where we play football. It's the best place on earth." The three mice began to jump all over each other, and Mitt, still confused, shouted "But how does this get me to the cheese-eating contest?"

Right then, a very large Canada goose named Falda floated down and the three mice began to cheer.

Wit, Lew, and Kaz were overjoyed that the goose had responded so quickly. They urged Mitt to climb up on her back, and he did so with little hesitation. With that, Falda lofted up and over the stadium as Mitt watched Wit, Lew, and Kaz below, waving their paws and tails in the silly way that cheddarhead mice will do. Mitt shouted to them, "I will see you again, I know I will!"

The large bird drew his wings in and out

with a gentle rhythm that lulled Mitt in and out of sleep. Falda flew southward, hoping to get Mitt to the Cheese Jamboree within the day. He was flying alone, which was not natural for a Canada goose, but he told Mitt he was often called upon for such duties, and was happy to be helpful. Mitt thought that the goose was kind and generous for doing so. He was relieved that he was finally on his way to the Jamboree. Mitt watched the cornfields below. They were tall now that it was late summer, and the rows looked like ribbons of green across a dark brown land.

Mitt was having such a pleasant ride that he hardly noticed the gentle rain that started to fall. It wasn't enough to slow the goose or throw him off course. At least, at first.

CHAPTER FIFTEEN
Bodil the Vulture

While Mitt and Falda were making their way through the rain, Stig was now in southern Wisconsin with Minn, making his way toward the Cheese Jamboree. He was near Devil's Lake State Park and needing to rest. He slumped down into a bed, weary from the journey and yet on the watch for trouble. Minn knew to watch for trouble, too, but the two were so exhausted, that they fell asleep.

The next thing Minn knew, the buck was upright, snorting, and step-by-step backing away slowly. He told Minn to act as if she were dead, and so Minn, now several big steps away from Stig, made herself as still as a statue. A timber rattlesnake was threatening the buck, making a loud hissing sound and preparing to strike one of them. Minn knew, in the way a threatened mouse will know, that she better do as the buck told her.

And that's when it happened.

The turkey vulture was Bodil, and she was watching from above. Waiting for an opportunity, she swooped in and grabbed Minn.

Her large black wings flapped with an awkward pace to get up and out of the forest canopy. Her face was red and narrow and her eyes shiny and small. She was an old vulture, and her senses were not as keen as they once were.

But Minn continued to play dead and the turkey vulture, catching an updraft, went soaring above the forest and rocky edges below. Bodil, as all turkey vultures do, would only eat dead mice, and thinking Minn was dead, held her tightly in her grasp. She was flying over Horicon Marsh when, all of sudden, Minn wiggled, and Bodil, not sure whether to feel frightened or freakish, dropped Minn toward the marsh below.

On the side of the marsh, Falda was resting with Mitt, pleasantly napping in the subtle tones of the summer sunset, listening to the sounds of common yellowthroat birds and red-winged blackbirds and the gentle purr of rivulets being made by the lifting and landing of whooping cranes and herons. While resting there, something came splashing into the water with a SWOOSH! The goose, being the helpful type, dashed out to see what it was, returning with a very small, weak, and drenched mouse in his bill.

Upon seeing the mouse, Mitt gave up his place and told the goose to warm her up. The goose did so while Mitt sat nearby and watched, not knowing the small mouse's name or how she dropped from the sky, or where she was going. All they knew, in the way that kind animals know, was that she needed help, and they were happy to lend it.

Minn warmed herself beneath the warm down of the goose. When she was dry, she poked her head out to see Mitt settled near Falda's wing. Mitt had gathered seeds from sedge grasses and placed them nearby so the half-drowned mouse would have food when she woke. Grateful for this, Minn began to eat eagerly and, gathering her strength, began to chatter about her journey.

Mitt and the goose listened closely. Minn told them all about Gerdie and her home

near Ely, and how she had been on such a long journey. She spoke about how Gerdie was the only mother she had ever known, and how they had become separated and that Gerdie was somewhere looking for her right now.

As she was speaking, something made Mitt feel very low. He thought about how he was so far from his mitten, and how all he had was the memory of his mother and father. He was feeling sorry for himself as Minn was still speaking.

"And that's why I'm on my way to win the cheese-eating contest at the Cheese Jamboree. That's the only way Gerdie will find me."

This made Mitt angry. "How dare she think she's going to the Cheese Jamboree to win the contest. I need to win. I need to do one good thing so I can find my way home," he thought. Mitt stared at Minn with a wave of jealousy. He noticed she was a white-footed mouse like he was, and seemed to have a strong will like he did. But even so, he did not want her to win.

Neither Mitt nor Minn sensed the great egret stalking up behind the nest, its long sharp yellow bill pointed right at Minn.

And then he took her. He held her in his bill and pushed off with his thin gray legs, lighting to the sky and coasting over and away from the marsh.

Mitt tried to grasp her, but it was no use. It was too late. His heart seemed to shrink in his body, leaving him feeling badly about his thoughts toward her. As he watched them go farther away, becoming smaller against the horizon, he felt a pull in his heart that told him there was something he liked about Minn, and now he would never see her again. She would never make it to the cheese-eating contest to find Gerdie, and it was his fault for wishing it so.

CHAPTER SIXTEEN
Minn's Ride

Falda began to squawk in the way a goose in a hurry will squawk, telling Mitt it was time to go. The pair lit to the sky, flying north. The egret was going north, too, but not following the same path. For some reason it felt the need to land again before swallowing Minn whole, and so spotted a beautiful garden in which to rest. As the egret came down, he began to twitch his wings wildly and kick his feet back and forth. Once on the ground, he dropped Minn so that he could fight the swarm of honey-bees he had landed into.

Minn knew she had to escape quickly and, spotting a tower of white boxes, made a run for it.

The boxes were stacked in neat layers and buzzing with sound. But even so, Minn's need for safety overwhelmed her natural instinct. She scrambled inside. All of a sudden, one great big honeybee landed on top of her head. "Hey, where do you think you're heading?" he quizzed her.

"I'm hiding," said Minn.

The bee replied, "Well, be on your way and be quick about it."

With that, Minn began to cry. She told him about how she was stolen by Rink the raven, and how Gerdie was out looking for her, and how she needed to get to the Cheese Jamboree because that is where Gerdie would be looking for her.

The honeybee, in the sweet way that honeybees do, understood why this would be important to such a mouse, and so spoke up.

"Cheese Jamboree? Stay with me. Mr. Johnson the beekeeper is bringing his honey to the Jamboree. Follow me and I will show you the way to his truck. You can hop in and ride there, he will never know." The honeybee continued, "But if I were you, I would get out of here before the queen comes down."

Minn was impressed that the honeybees had their own queen and followed the order swiftly. She poked her nose outside to make certain the egret was gone and, once satisfied, followed the bee through the meadow and up to the farmer's home.

CHAPTER SEVENTEEN

The Cheese Jamboree

The truck rolled along and it was an easy ride for Minn, who simply hid in one of the boxes filled with honey jars. When the truck came to a stop and the farmer opened the door, Minn raced out. Right away, Minn saw two large tents with red-and-white-striped sides and three bigger tents with tops that were blue with yellow checkers. There were people milling everywhere, and so Minn knew right away to keep herself out of sight while looking for Gerdie.

The smell of sweet and spicy sausage cooking over wood smoke pulled her along, and so she followed the smell.

The food tent had long rows of picnic tables inside, and one long table where people were gathering to get food such as potato chips and cheese curds, bratwurst and hot dogs, snow cones and candies, fresh squeezed lemonade and soda. There was one spot where people were getting big red cups of cold, sweet milk and chocolate chip cookies warm from the oven. To Minn, this wasn't a Cheese Jamboree, this was heaven.

As Minn snacked on cracker crumbs, she spotted all types of other mice running around like her, snapping up morsels and feasting on the leftovers.

This was a good place to be, and Minn knew Gerdie must be near, as she liked to sample all sorts of foods and cheeses. But first she had to find the cheese-eating contest because that is where Gerdie would most likely be.

At the same time, the goose landed on the grounds of the Cheese Jamboree and told Mitt that he would now be able to go do one good thing, and then find his way home. With that, Falda left, and Mitt began his search for the cheese-eating contest. His thoughts turned to Minn, as all the excitement of the Jamboree made him feel sorry that she had been grabbed by the egret and would not be able to find her Gerdie. But as sad as that made Mitt feel, there was just a little part of him that was happy not to have the competition.

CHAPTER EIGHTEEN

The Cheese-Eating Contest

As Mitt sat there lost in his thoughts, a bright sort of music began to play from the bandshell, and pairs of people in colorful dresses and neatly pressed slacks stepped onto the wood floor to dance. The accordion player seemed to jump back and forth as he played the polka, and the dancers hop-skipped their way across the dance floor. Mitt saw the

Mitt was too tired to disagree, and so settled into the basket with Minn. And then, as they were beginning to leave, one of the Jersey cows spoke up in the low, cautious way a smart cow will speak when certain of what they are about to say. Her name was Lilka and she was the oldest of them all.

"You are a brother and sister who were separated from each other long ago?" Then nodding toward Mitt, said, "You came from a red wool mitten in the woods?" And then to Minn, "And you came from a basket of cherries brought to Minnesota?"

Mitt and Minn nodded.

Lilka continued, "I know your parents."

"What?" exclaimed Mitt and Minn in the hurried way that a pair of confused mice will exclaim. "A mother? A father?"

And then Lilka told the story while Gerdie, Mitt, and Minn listened carefully.

"The farm where I live is beautiful and large and there are many barns and many gardens. My barn is white and long and has many cows, and many sheep, and many mice. One of the mice that lives there is Viktor. One night a very long time ago, Viktor came in with two white-footed mice, like you, and helped them find crumbs to eat and a warm place to sleep. They were wet and weary, thin and confused. For days the mother mouse kept repeating, 'The basket, the mittens, my babies! The basket, the mittens, my babies!' Father mouse would comfort her and tell her they would not stop searching until they found them."

Lilka went on, "The Jamboree is over. Everyone is packing up and soon we will be going back to Illinois. If you climb up

and hang on tightly, I will take you to my farm, and you can meet Viktor. He helped your mother and father find another place to live nearby, and he will help you reach them."

Mitt and Minn gave each other a long, hard stare, bonded by the news they now shared. A mother and a father. All of a sudden the red wool mitten didn't matter to Mitt as much as it had before because, in some small way, he was truly about to find his way home.

CHAPTER TWENTY-TWO

Home

Gerdie was silent. For such a long time she had been the only mother Minn had ever known. But being kind and wise in the ways of animals, she knew this was important news for Mitt and Minn.

Minn wanted both. She wanted to go home with Gerdie, and she wanted to find her parents. But she couldn't have both.

Deep inside, Gerdie wanted to beg Minn to come home with her. She wanted to say *enda barn, kart barn,* and hold her in the cup of her hands. She wanted to put Minn to sleep in her little dresser drawer bed and make her treats of oatmeal cakes and cream. Illinois was a big place for such little mice and Gerdie knew it would be dangerous for both of them. ·

The silence filled the barn like a cloud fills with rain. Gerdie thought about her own son who she hadn't seen for such a long time. She had always hoped that someday he would come find her. Understanding the courage that it takes to do something so

brave, Gerdie swelled with great respect and pride for Minn and Mitt. Then she spoke. "You go. Go find your mother and your father."

But before she left she took a folded piece of paper out of her jacket pocket. It was the bulletin for the Cheese Jamboree that Mitt and Minn had both seen so long ago.

She laid it out flat on a hay bale so Mitt and Minn could see it. Without speaking, she pointed her finger to just a couple of words.

To **All** Willing:
Heart of Wisconsin Cheese Jamboree
Please **Do** Come!
One First Prize Cheese Contest
Good Treats and Games
Cheese Smorgasbord, **Try** Any Thing You Like!

And then she left.

All Heart. Do Try.

Mitt and Minn looked at each other, brave in the new thought that they were family, and brave in their quest to search for their mother and father. They just didn't know how hard it would be.

And so that is how it came to be that a pair of mice came riding into Illinois on the back of an old Jersey cow one warm late summer day. Now that they had found each other, they had one more quest ahead of them, and it would take both of them, each full of heart, to succeed.

COMING SOON...

Mitt & Minn's Illinois Adventure

In 2006, Mitten Press started a series of chapter books about a lively pair of white-footed mice. Mitt, the Michigan mouse lives in the woods of northern Michigan near Cheboygan. When his beloved mitten home is lost, he embarks on a journey around the state to try to find it. At the same time in Minnesota, a raven snatches spunky little Minn from the cabin where she lives with her human friend Gerdie. She too will face many challenges as she attempts to find her way home. In this Book Three, both mice head to Wisconsin and compete in a cheese-eating contest at the Cheese Jamboree.

Readers are sure to learn more than a little about the states in the midwest as they travel along with these clever mice!

Book One: *Mitt, the Michigan Mouse*
ISBN: 978-1-58726-303-3

Book Two: *Minn from Minnesota*
ISBN: 978-1-58726-304-0

Book Three: *Mitt & Minn at the Wisconsin Cheese Jamboree*
ISBN: 978-1-58726-305-7

Book Four: *Mitt & Minn's Illinois Adventure*
ISBN: 978-1-58726-306-4

Join Mitt and Minn's Midwest Readers by sending your email address to the publisher at ljohnson@mittenpress.com. You will receive updates as new books in the series are completed and fun activities to challenge what you know about the Midwest states.

www.mittenpress.com

BOUNDARY
WATERS CANOE
AREA

Minn

SILVER
BAY

HAYWARD

CHEESE
JAMBOREE
ADMIT
ONE

CHEESE
DEE
ADMIT
ONE

N NE S O T A

W

ILLINOIS
MISSOURI

I O W A

CAPE GIRARDEAU